This book belongs to:

....

....

A BEDTIME STORY-BOOK

THE

ADVENTURES OF

Jimmy
SKUNK

THORNTON W. BURGESS

LITTLE, BROWN AND COMPANY

BOSTON   TORONTO

Republished in 1987

Library of Congress Cataloging-in-Publication Data

Burgess, Thornton W. (Thornton Waldo), 1874-1965.
The adventures of Jimmy Skunk.

(A Bedtime story-book)
Summary: When the Smiling Pool hear their homes
dries up, Jimmy Skunk and his forest friends
set out to find the cause.

[1. Skunks–Fiction. 2. Animals–Fiction]
I. Cady, Harrison, 1877-   ill.   II. Title.
III. Series.
PZ7.B917Ac   1987   [E]   87-3090
ISBN 0-316-11627-0 (pbk.)

Illustrations by Harrison Cady

PRINTED AND BOUND IN CANADA

CONTENTS

CONTENTS

THE ADVENTURES OF JIMMY SKUNK

I

PETER RABBIT PLANS A JOKE

The Imp of Mischief, woe is me,
Is always busy as a bee.

THAT is why so many people are forever getting into trouble. He won't keep still. No, Sir, he won't keep still unless he is made to. Once let him get started there is no knowing where he will stop. Peter Rabbit had just seen Jimmy Skunk disappear inside an old barrel, lying on its side at the top of the hill, and at once the Imp of Mischief be-

gan to whisper to Peter. Of course
Peter shouldn't have listened. Certainly not. But he did. You know
Peter dearly loves a joke when it is on
some one else. He sat right where he
was and watched to see if Jimmy would
come out of the barrel. Jimmy didn't
come out, and after a little Peter stole
over to the barrel and peeped inside.
There was Jimmy Skunk curled up for
a nap.

Peter tiptoed away very softly. All
the time the Imp of Mischief was whispering to him that this was a splendid
chance to play a joke on Jimmy. You
know it is very easy to play a joke on
any one who is asleep. Peter doesn't
often have a chance to play a joke on
Jimmy Skunk. It isn't a very safe
thing to do, not if Jimmy is awake. No
one knows that better than Peter. He
sat down some distance from the barrel

but where he could keep an eye on it. Then he went into a brown study, which is one way of saying that he thought very hard. He wanted to play a joke on Jimmy, but like most jokers he didn't want the joke to come back on himself. In fact, he felt that it would be a great deal better for him if Jimmy shouldn't know that he had anything to do with the joke.

As he sat there in a brown study, he happened to glance over on the Green Meadows and there he saw something red. He looked very hard, and in a minute he saw that it was Reddy Fox. Right away, Peter's nimble wits began to plan how he could use Reddy Fox to play a joke on Jimmy. All in a flash an idea came to him, an idea that made him laugh right out. You see, the Imp of Mischief was very, very busy whispering to Peter.

"If Reddy were only up here, I believe I could do it, and it would be a joke on Reddy as well as on Jimmy," thought Peter, and laughed right out again.

"What are you laughing at?" asked a voice. It was the voice of Sammy Jay.

Right away a plan for getting Reddy up there flashed into Peter's head. He would get Sammy angry, and that would make Sammy scream. Reddy would be sure to come up there to see what Sammy Jay was making such a fuss about. Sammy, you know, is very quick-tempered. No one knows this better than Peter. So instead of replying politely to Sammy, as he should have done, Peter spoke crossly:

"Fly away, Sammy, fly away! It is no business of yours what I am laughing at," said he.

Right away Sammy's quick temper flared up. He began to call Peter names, and Peter answered back. This angered Sammy still more, and as he always screams when he is angry, he was soon making such a racket that Reddy Fox down on the Green Meadows couldn't help but hear it. Peter saw him lift his head to listen. In a few minutes he began to trot that way. He was coming to find out what that fuss was about. Peter knew that Reddy wouldn't come straight up there. That isn't Reddy's way. He would steal around back of the old stone wall on the edge of the Old Orchard, which was back of Peter, and would try to see what was going on without being seen himself.

"As soon as he sees me he will think that at last he has a chance to catch me," thought Peter. "I shall have to

run my very fastest, but if everything
goes right, he will soon forget all about
me. I do hope that the noise Sammy
Jay is making will not waken Jimmy
Skunk and bring him out to see what is
going on.''

So with one eye on the barrel where
Jimmy Skunk was taking a nap, and the
other eye on the old stone wall behind
which he expected Reddy Fox to come
stealing up, Peter waited and didn't
mind in the least the names that Sammy
Jay was calling him.

II

PETER MAKES A FLYING JUMP

To risk your life unless there's need
Is downright foolishness indeed.

NEVER forget that. Never **do** such a crazy thing as Peter Rabbit was doing. What was he doing? Why, he was running the risk of being caught by Reddy Fox all for the sake of a joke. Did you ever hear of anything more foolish? Yet Peter was no different from a lot of people who every day risk their lives in the most careless and heedless ways just to save a few minutes of time or for some other equally foolish reason. The fact is, Peter didn't stop to think what dreadful thing might happen if his plans didn't work out as he intended.

He didn't once think of little Mrs. Peter over in the dear Old Briar-patch and how she would feel if he never came home again. That's the trouble with thoughtlessness; it never remembers other people.

All the time that Reddy Fox was creeping along behind the old stone wall on the edge of the Old Orchard, Peter knew just where he was, though Reddy didn't know that. If he had known it, he would have suspected one of Peter's tricks.

"He'll peep over that wall, and just as soon as he sees me, he will feel sure that this time he will catch me," thought Peter. "He will steal along to that place where the wall is lowest and will jump over it right there. I must be ready to jump the very second he does."

It all happened just as Peter had expected. While seeming to be paying no

attention to anything but to Sammy
Jay, he kept his eyes on that low place
in the old wall, and presently he saw
Reddy's sharp nose, as Reddy peeped
over to make sure that he was still there.
The instant that sharp nose dropped out
of sight, Peter made ready to run for
his life. A second later, Reddy leaped
over the wall, and Peter was off as hard
as he could go, with Reddy almost at his
heels. Sammy Jay, who had been so
busy calling Peter names that he hadn't
seen Reddy at all, forgot all about his
quarrel with Peter.

"Go it, Peter! Go it!" he screamed
excitedly. That was just like Sammy.

Peter did go it. He had to. He ran
with all his might. Reddy grinned as
he saw Peter start towards the Green
Meadows. It was a long way to the
dear Old Briar-patch, and Reddy
didn't have any doubt at all that he

would catch Peter before he got there.
He watched sharply for Peter to dodge
and try to get back to the old stone wall.
He didn't mean to let Peter do that.
But Peter didn't even try. He ran
straight for the edge of the hill above
the Green Meadows. Then, for the first
time, Reddy noticed an old barrel there
lying on its side.

"I wonder if he thinks he can hide in
that," thought Reddy, and grinned
again, for he remembered that he had
passed that old barrel a few days before, and that one end was open while
the other end was closed. "If he tries
that, I will get him without the trouble
of much of a chase," thought Reddy,
and chuckled.

Lipperty-lipperty-lip ran Peter, lipperty-lipperty-lip, Reddy right at his
heels! To Sammy Jay it looked as if
in a few more jumps Reddy certainly

would catch Peter. "Go it, Peter!
Oh, go it! Go it!" screamed Sammy,
for in spite of his quarrels with Peter,
he didn't want to see him come to any
real harm.

Just as he reached the old barrel,
Reddy was so close to him that Peter
was almost sure that he could feel
Reddy's breath. Then Peter made a
splendid flying jump right over the old
barrel and kept on down the hill, lipperty-lipperty-lip, as fast as ever he
could, straight for an old house of
Johnny Chuck's of which he knew.
When he reached it, he turned to see
what was happening behind him, for he
knew by the screaming of Sammy Jay
and by other sounds that a great deal
was happening. In fact, he suspected
that the joke which he had planned was
working out just as he had hoped it
would.

III

WHAT HAPPENED AT THE OLD BARREL

PETER RABBIT'S jump over the old barrel on the edge of the hill was unexpected to Reddy Fox. In fact, Reddy was so close on Peter's heels that he had no thought of anything but catching Peter. He was running so fast that when Peter made his flying jump over the barrel, Reddy did not have time to jump too, and he ran right smack bang against that old barrel. Now you remember that that barrel was right on the edge of the hill. When Reddy ran against it, he hit it so hard that he rolled it over, and of course that started it down the hill. You know a barrel is a very rolly sort of thing, and once it has started down a hill, nothing can stop it.

It was just so this time. Reddy Fox had no more than picked himself up when the barrel was half way down the hill and going faster and faster. It bounced along over the ground, and every time it hit a little hummock it seemed to jump right up in the air. And all the time it was making the strangest noises. Reddy quite forgot the smarting sore places where he had bumped into the barrel. He simply stood and stared at the runaway.

"As I live," he exclaimed, "I believe there was some one in that old barrel!" There was. You remember that Jimmy Skunk had curled up in there for a nap. Now Jimmy was awake, very much awake. You see, for once in his life he was moving fast, very much faster than ever he had moved before since he was born. And it wasn't at all comfortable. No, Sir, it wasn't at all a comfortable way in which to travel. He went over and over so fast that it made him dizzy. First he was right side up and then wrong side up, so fast that he couldn't tell which side up he was. And every time that old barrel jumped when it went over a hummock, Jimmy was tossed up so that he hit whatever part of the barrel happened to be above him. Of course, he couldn't get out, because he was rolled over and over so fast that he didn't have a chance to try.

Now Reddy didn't know who was in the barrel. He just knew by the sounds that some one was. So he started down the hill after the barrel to see what would happen when it stopped. All the time Peter Rabbit was dancing about in the greatest excitement, but taking the greatest care to keep close to that old house of Johnny Chuck's so as to pop into it in case of danger. He saw that Reddy Fox had quite forgotten all about him in his curiosity as to who was in the barrel, and he chuckled as he thought of what might happen when the barrel stopped rolling and Reddy found out. Sammy Jay was flying overhead, screaming enough to split his throat. Altogether, is was quite the most exciting thing Peter had ever seen.

Now it just happened that Old Man Coyote had started to cross the Green Meadows right at the foot of the hill just as the barrel started down. Of course, he heard the noise and looked up to see what it meant. When he saw that barrel rushing right down at him, it frightened him so that he just gave one yelp and started for the Old Pasture like a gray streak. He gave Peter a chance to see just how fast he can run, and

Peter made up his mind right then that he never would run a race with Old Man Coyote.

Down at the bottom of the hill was a big stone, and when the barrel hit this, the hoops broke, and the barrel fell all apart. Peter decided that it was high time for him to get out of sight. So he dodged into the old house of Johnny Chuck and lay low in the doorway, where he could watch. He saw Jimmy Skunk lay perfectly still, and a great fear crept into his heart. Had Jimmy been killed? He hadn't once thought of what might happen to Jimmy when he planned that joke. But presently Jimmy began to wave first one leg and then another, as if to make sure that he had some legs left. Then slowly he rolled over and got on to his feet. Peter breathed a sigh of relief.

IV

JIMMY SKUNK IS VERY MAD INDEED

When Jimmy Skunk is angry
Then every one watch out!
It's better far at such a time
To be nowhere about.

JIMMY SKUNK was angry this time and no mistake. He was just plain *mad,* and when Jimmy Skunk feels that way, no one wants to be very near him. You know he is one of the very best-natured little fellows in the world ordinarily. He minds his own business, and if no one interferes with him, he interferes with no one. But once he is aroused and feels that he hasn't been treated fairly, look out for him!

And this time Jimmy was mad clear through, as he got to his feet and shook himself to see that he was all there. I don't know that any one could blame him. To be wakened from a comfortable nap by being rolled over and over and shaken nearly to death as Jimmy had been by that wild ride down the hill in the old barrel was enough to make any one mad. So he really is not to be blamed for feeling as he did.

Now Jimmy can never be accused of being stupid. He knew that an old barrel which has been lying in one place for a long time doesn't move of its own accord. He knew that that barrel couldn't possibly have started off down the hill unless some one had made it start, and he didn't have a doubt in the world that whoever had done it, had known that he was inside and had done it to make him uncomfortable. So just as soon as he had made sure that he was really alive and quite whole, he looked about to see who could have played such a trick on him.

The first person he saw was Reddy Fox. In fact, Reddy was right close at hand. You see, he had raced down the hill after the barrel to see who was in it when he heard the strange noises coming from it as it rolled and bounded down. If Reddy had known that it was Jimmy Skunk, he would have been quite content to remain at the top of the hill. But he didn't know, and if the truth be known, he had hopes that it might prove to be some one who would furnish him with a good breakfast. So, quite out of breath with running, Reddy arrived at the place where the old barrel had broken to pieces just as Jimmy got to his feet.

Now when Jimmy Skunk is angry, he

doesn't bite and he doesn't scratch. You know Old Mother Nature has provided him with a little bag of perfume which Jimmy doesn't object to in the least, but which makes most people want to hold their noses and run. He never uses it, excepting when he is angry or in danger, but when he does use it, his enemies always turn tail and run. That is why he is afraid of no one, and why every one respects Jimmy and his rights.

He used it now, and he didn't waste any time about it. He threw some of that perfume right in the face of Reddy Fox before Reddy had a chance to turn or to say a word.

"Take that!" snapped Jimmy Skunk. "Perhaps it will teach you not to play tricks on your honest neighbors!"

Poor Reddy! Some of that perfume got in his eyes and made them smart dreadfully. In fact, for a little while he couldn't see at all. And then the smell of it was so strong that it made him quite sick. He rolled over and over on the ground, choking and gasping and rubbing his eyes. Jimmy Skunk just stood and looked on, and there wasn't a bit of pity in his eyes.

"How do you like that?" said he. "You thought yourself very smart, rolling me down hill in a barrel, didn't you? You might have broken my neck."

"I didn't know you were in that barrel, and I didn't mean to roll it down the hill anyway," whined Reddy, when he could get his voice.

"Huh!" snorted Jimmy Skunk, who didn't believe a word of it.

"I didn't. Honestly I didn't," protested Reddy. "I ran against the barrel by accident, chasing Peter Rabbit. I didn't have any idea that any one was in it."

"Huh!" said Jimmy Skunk again. "If you were chasing Peter Rabbit, where is he now?"

Reddy had to confess he didn't know. He was nowhere in sight, and he certainly hadn't had time to reach the dear Old Briar-patch. Jimmy looked this way and that way, but there was no sign of Peter Rabbit.

"Huh!" said he again, turning his back on Reddy Fox and walking away with a great deal of dignity.

V

REDDY FOX SNEAKS AWAY

TO sneak away is to steal away trying to keep out of sight of everybody, and is usually done only by those who for some reason or other are ashamed to be seen. Just as soon as Reddy Fox could see after Jimmy Skunk had thrown that terrible perfume in Reddy's face he started for the Green Forest. He wanted to get away by himself. But he didn't trot with his head up and his big plumey tail carried proudly as is usual with him. No indeed. Instead he hung his head, and his handsome tail was dropped between his legs; he was the very picture of shame. You see that terrible per-

fume which Jimmy Skunk had thrown
at him clung to his red coat and he knew
that he couldn't get rid of it, not for a
long time anyway. And he knew, too,
that wherever he went his neighbors
would hold their noses and make fun of
him, and that no one would have anything to do with him. So he sneaked
away across the Green Meadows
towards the Green Forest and he felt
too sick and mean and unhappy to even
be angry with Sammy Jay, who was
making fun of him and saying that he
had got no more than he deserved.

Poor Reddy! He didn't know what
to do or where to go. He couldn't go
home, for old Granny Fox would drive
him out of the house. She had warned
him time and again never to provoke
Jimmy Skunk, and he knew that she
never would forgive him if he should
bring that terrible perfume near their

home. He knew, too, that it would not be long before all the little people of the Green Forest and the Green Meadows would know what had happened to him. Sammy Jay would see to that. He knew just how they would point at him and make fun of him. He would never hear the last of it. He felt as if he never, never would be able to hold his head and his tail up again. Every few minutes he stopped to roll over and over on the ground trying to get rid of that dreadful perfume.

When he reached the Green Forest he hurried over to the Laughing Brook to wash out his eyes. It was just his luck to have Billy Mink come along while he was doing this. Billy didn't need to be told what had happened. "Phew!" he exclaimed, holding on to his nose. Then he turned and hurried beyond the reach of that perfume. There he stopped and made fun of Reddy Fox and said all the provoking things he could think of. Reddy took no notice at all. He felt too miserable to quarrel.

After he had washed his face he felt better. Water wouldn't take away the awful smell, but it did take away the smart from his eyes. Then he tried to plan what to do next.

"The only thing I can do is to get as far away from everybody as I can," thought he. "I guess I'll have to go up to the Old Pasture to live for a while."

So he started for the Old Pasture, keeping as much out of sight as possible. On the way he remembered that Old Man Coyote lived there. Of course it would never do to go near Old Man Coyote's home for if he smelled that awful perfume and discovered that he, Reddy, was the cause of it he would certainly drive him out of the Old Pasture

and then where could he go? So Reddy
went to the loneliest part of the Old
Pasture and crept into an old house that
he and Granny had dug there long ago
when they had been forced to live in the
Old Pasture in the days when Farmer
Brown's boy and Bowser the Hound
had hunted them for stealing chickens.
There he stretched himself out and was
perfectly miscrable.

"It wouldn't be so bad if I had really
been to blame, but I wasn't. I didn't
know Jimmy Skunk was in that barrel
and I didn't mean to start it rolling
down the hill anyway," he muttered.
"It was all an accident and—" He
stopped and into his yellow eyes crept
a look of suspicion. "I wonder," said
he slowly, "if Peter Rabbit knew that
Jimmy Skunk was there and planned to
get me into all this trouble. I wonder."

VI

PETER RABBIT DOESN'T ENJOY HIS JOKE

 LL the time that Jimmy Skunk was punishing Reddy Fox for rolling him down hill in a barrel, and while Reddy was sneaking away to the Green Forest to get out of sight, Peter Rabbit was lying low in the old house of Johnny Chuck, right near the place where Jimmy Skunk's wild ride had come to an end. It had been a great relief to Peter when he had seen Jimmy Skunk get to his feet, and he knew that Jimmy hadn't been hurt in that wild ride. Lying flat in the doorway of Johnny Chuck's old house, Peter could see all that went on without being

seen himself, and he could hear all that
was said.

He chuckled as he saw Reddy Fox
come up and his eyes were popping right
out with excitement as he waited for
what would happen next. He felt sure
that Reddy Fox was in for something
unpleasant, and he was glad. Of
course, that wasn't a bit nice of Peter.
Right down in his heart Peter knew it,
but he had been chased so often by
Reddy and given so many dreadful
frights, that he felt now that he was getting even. So he chuckled as he waited
for what was to happen. Suddenly that
chuckle broke right off in the middle,
and Peter cried "Ouch!" He had felt
a pain as if a hot needle had been thrust
into him. It made him almost jump out
of the doorway. But he remembered in
time that it would never, never do for
him to show himself outside, for right

away Reddy Fox and Jimmy Skunk would suspect that he had had something to do with that wild ride of Jimmy's in the barrel. So it would not do to show himself now. No, indeed!

All he could do was to kick and squirm and twist his head around to see what was happening. It didn't take long to find out. Even as he looked, he felt another sharp pain which brought another "Ouch!" from him and made him kick harder than ever. Two very angry little insects were just getting ready to sting him again, and more were coming. They were Yellow Jackets, which you know belong to the wasp family and carry very sharp little lances in their tails. The fact is, this old house of Johnny Chuck's had been deserted so long the Yellow Jackets had decided that as no one else was using it, they would, and they had begun to build their home just inside the hall.

Poor Peter! What could he do? He didn't dare go out, and he simply couldn't stay where he was. Whatever he did must be done quickly, for it looked to him as if a regular army of Yellow Jackets was coming, and those little lances they carried were about the most painful things he knew of. By this time he had lost all interest in what was going on outside. There was quite enough going on inside; too much, in fact. He remembered that Johnny Chuck digs his house deep down in the ground. He looked down the long hall. It was dark down there. Perhaps if he went down there, these angry little warriors wouldn't follow him. It was worth trying, anyway.

So Peter scrambled to his feet and scurried down the long hall, and as he ran, he cried "Ouch! Ouch! Oh! Ohoo!" Those sharp little lances were very busy, and there was no way of fighting back. At the end of the long hall was a snug little room, very dark but cool and comfortable. It was just as he had hoped; the Yellow Jackets did not follow him down there. They had driven him away from their home, which was right near the entrance, and they were satisfied.

But what a fix he was in! What a dreadful fix! He ached and smarted all over. My goodness, how he did smart! And to get out he would have to go right past the Yellow Jacket home again.

"Oh, dear, I wish I had never thought of such a joke," moaned Peter, trying in vain to find a comfortable position. "I guess I am served just right."

I rather think he was, don't you?

VII

SAMMY JAY DOES SOME GUESSING

SAMMY JAY is a queer fellow. Although he is a scamp and dearly loves to make trouble for his neighbors, he is always ready to take their part when others make trouble for them. Many are the times he has given them warning of danger. This is one reason they are quite willing to overlook his own shortcomings. So, though in many ways he is no better than Reddy Fox, he dearly loves to upset Reddy's plans and is very apt to rejoice when Reddy gets into trouble. Of course, being right there, he saw all that happened when Reddy ran against the old barrel at the top of the hill and sent it rolling.

He had been quite as much surprised as
Reddy to find that there was some one
inside, and he had followed Reddy to
see who it was. So, of course, he had
seen what happened to Reddy.

Now, instead of being sorry for
Reddy, he had openly rejoiced. It
seems to be just that way with a great
many people. They like to see others
who are considered very smart get into
trouble. So Sammy had laughed and
made fun of poor Reddy. In the first
place it was very exciting, and Sammy
dearly loves excitement. And then it
would make such a splendid story to
tell, and no one likes to carry tales more
than does Sammy Jay. He watched
Reddy sneak away to the Green Forest,
and Jimmy Skunk slowly walk away in
a very dignified manner. Then Sammy
flew back to the Old Orchard to spread
the news among the little people there.

It wasn't until he reached the Old Orchard that he remembered Peter Rabbit. Instead of flying about telling every one what had happened to Jimmy Skunk and Reddy Fox, he found a comfortable perch in an old apple-tree and was strangely silent. The fact is, Sammy Jay was doing some hard thinking. He had suddenly begun to wonder. It had popped into that shrewd little head of his that it was very strange how suddenly Peter Rabbit had disappeared.

"Of course," thought Sammy, "Jimmy Skunk is sure that Reddy rolled that barrel down hill purposely, and I don't wonder that he does think so. But I saw it all, and I know that it was all an accident so far as Reddy was concerned. I didn't know that Jimmy was in that barrel, and Reddy couldn't have known it, because he didn't come up here until after I did. But Peter Rabbit may have known. Why did Peter run so that he would have to jump over that barrel when he could have run right past it?

"Of course, he may have thought that if he could make Reddy run right slam bang against that barrel it would stop Reddy long enough to give him a chance to get away. That would have been pretty smart of Peter and quite like him. But somehow I have a feeling that he knew all the time that Jimmy Skunk was taking a nap inside and that something was bound to happen if he was disturbed. The more I think of it, the more I believe that Peter did know and that he planned the whole thing. If he did, it was one of the smartest tricks I ever heard of. I didn't think Peter had it in him. It was rather hard on Jimmy Skunk, but

it got rid of Reddy Fox for a while.
He won't dare show his face around
here for a long time. That means that
Peter will have one less worry on his
mind. Hello! Here comes Jimmy
Skunk. I'll ask him a few questions.''

Jimmy came ambling along in his
usual lazy manner. He had quite recovered his good nature. He felt that
he was more than even with Reddy Fox,
and as he was none the worse for his
wild ride in the barrel, he had quite forgotten that he had lost his temper.

"Hello, Jimmy. Have you seen Peter Rabbit this morning?" cried Sammy
Jay.

Jimmy looked up and grinned.
"Yes," said he. "I saw him up here
early this morning. Why?"

"Did he see you go into that old barrel?" persisted Sammy.

"I don't know," confessed Jimmy.

"He may have. What have you got on your mind, Sammy Jay?"

"Nothing much, only Reddy Fox was chasing him when he ran against that barrel and sent you rolling down the hill," replied Sammy.

Jimmy pricked up his ears. "Then Reddy didn't do it purposely!" he exclaimed.

"No," replied Sammy. "He didn't do it purposely. I am quite sure that he didn't know you were in it. But how about Peter Rabbit? I am wondering. And I'm doing a little guessing, too."

VIII

JIMMY SKUNK LOOKS FOR PETER

JIMMY SKUNK looked very hard at Sammy Jay. Sammy Jay looked very hard at Jimmy Skunk. Then Sammy slowly shut one eye and as slowly opened it again. It was a wink.

"You mean," said Jimmy Skunk, "that you guess that Peter Rabbit knew that I was in that barrel, and that he jumped over it so as to make Reddy Fox run against it. Is that it?"

Sammy Jay said nothing, but winked again. Jimmy grinned. Then he looked thoughtful. "I wonder," said he slowly, "if Peter did it so as to gain time to get away from Reddy Fox."

"I wonder," said Sammy Jay.

"And I wonder if he did it just to get Reddy into trouble," continued Jimmy.

"I wonder," repeated Sammy Jay.

"And I wonder if he did it for a joke, a double joke on Reddy and myself," Jimmy went on, scratching his head thoughtfully.

"I wonder," said Sammy Jay once more, and burst out laughing.

Now Jimmy Skunl. has a very shrewd little head on his shoulders. "So that is your guess, is it? Well, I wouldn't be a bit surprised if you are right," said he, nodding his head. "I think I will go look for Peter. I think he needs a lesson. Jokes that put other people in danger or make them uncomfortable can have no excuse. My neck might have been broken in that wild ride down the hill, and certainly I was made most uncomfortable. I felt as if everything inside me was shaken out of place and all mixed up. Even now my stomach feels a bit queer, as if it might not be just where it ought to be. By the way, what became of Peter after he jumped over the barrel?"

Sammy shook his head. "I don't know," he confessed. "You see, it was very exciting when that barrel started rolling, and we knew by the sounds that there was some one inside it. I guess Reddy Fox forgot all about Peter. I know I did. And when the barrel broke to pieces against that stone down there, and you and Reddy faced each other, it was still more exciting. After it was over, I looked for Peter, but he was no-where in sight. He hadn't had time to reach the Old Briar-patch. I really would like to know myself what became of him."

Jimmy Skunk turned and looked down the hill. Then in his usual slow

way he started back towards the broken
barrel.

"Where are you going?" asked
Sammy.

"To look for Peter Rabbit," replied
Jimmy. "I want to ask him a few questions."

Jimmy Skunk ambled along down the
hill. At first he was very angry as he
thought of what Peter had done, and he
made up his mind that Peter should be
taught a lesson he would never forget.
But as he ambled along, the funny side
of the whole affair struck him, for
Jimmy Skunk has a great sense of hu-
mor, and before he reached the bottom
of the hill his anger had all gone and
he was chuckling.

"I'm sorry if I did Reddy Fox an
injustice," thought he, "but he makes
so much trouble for other people that I
guess no one else will be sorry. He isn't

likely to bother any one for some time.
Peter really ought to be punished, but
somehow I don't feel so much like punishing him as I did. I'll just give him
a little scare and let the scamp off with
that. Now, I wonder where he can be.
I have an idea he isn't very far away.
Let me see. Seems to me I remember
an old house of Johnny Chuck's not very
far from here. I'll have a look in that."

IX

JIMMY SKUNK was smiling as he
ambled towards the old house of
Johnny Chuck near the foot of the
hill. There was no one near to see him,
and this made him smile still more.
You see, the odor of that perfume which
he had thrown at Reddy Fox just a little while before was very, very strong
there, and Jimmy knew that until that
had disappeared no one would come near
the place because it was so unpleasant
for every one. To Jimmy himself it
wasn't unpleasant at all, and he couldn't
understand why other people disliked it
so. He had puzzled over that a great

deal. He was glad that it was so, because on account of it every one treated him with respect and took special pains not to quarrel with him.

"I guess it's a good thing that Old Mother Nature didn't make us all alike," said he to himself. "I think there must be something the matter with their noses, and I suppose they think there is something the matter with mine. But there isn't. Not a thing. Hello! There is Johnny Chuck's old house just ahead of me. Now we will see what we shall see."

He walked softly as he drew near to the old house. If Peter was way down inside, it wouldn't matter how he approached. But if Peter should happen to be only just inside the doorway, he might take it into his head to run if he should hear footsteps, particularly if those footsteps were not heavy enough to

be those of Reddy or Granny Fox or Old
Man Coyote. Jimmy didn't intend to
give Peter a chance to do any such thing.
If Peter once got outside that old house,
his long legs would soon put him beyond
Jimmy's reach, and Jimmy knew it. If
he was to give Peter the fright that he
had made up his mind to give him, he
would first have to get him where he
couldn't run away. So Jimmy walked
as softly as he knew how and approached the old house in such a way as
to keep out of sight of Peter, should he
happen to be lying so as to look out of
the doorway.

At last he reached a position where
with one jump he could land right on the
doorstep. He waited a few minutes and
cocked his head on one side to listen.
There wasn't a sound to tell him whether
Peter was there or not. Then lightly
he jumped over to the doorstep and

looked in at the doorway. There was
no Peter to be seen.

"If he is here, he is way down inside,"
thought Jimmy. "I wonder if he
really is here. I think I'll look about a
bit before I go in."

Now the doorstep was of sand, as
Johnny Chuck's doorsteps always are.
Almost at once Jimmy chuckled. There
were Peter's tracks, and they pointed
straight towards the inside of Johnny
Chuck's old house. Jimmy looked carefully, but not a single track pointing the
other way could he find. Then he
chuckled again. "The scamp is here
all right," he muttered. "He hid here
and watched all that happened and then
decided to lie low and wait until he was
sure that the way was clear and no one
would see him." In this Jimmy was
partly right and partly wrong, as you
and I know.

He stared down the long dark doorway a minute. Then he made up his mind. "I'll go down and make Peter a call, and I won't bother to knock," he chuckled, and poked his head inside the doorway. But that was as far as Jimmy Skunk went. Yes, Sir, that was just as far as Jimmy Skunk went. You see, no sooner did he start to enter that old house of Johnny Chuck's than he was met by a lot of those Yellow Jackets, and they were in a very bad temper.

Jimmy Skunk knows all about Yellow Jackets and the sharp little lances they carry in their tails; he has the greatest respect for them. He backed out in a hurry and actually hurried away to a safe distance. Then he sat down to think. After a little he began to chuckle again. "I know what happened," said he, talking to himself. "Peter Rabbit popped into that doorway. Those Yellow Jackets just naturally got after him. He didn't dare come out for fear of Reddy Fox and me, and so he went on down to Jimmy Chuck's old bedroom, and he's down there now, wondering how ever he is to get out without getting stung. I reckon I don't need to scare Peter to pay him for that joke. I reckon he's been punished already."

X

PETER RABBIT IS MOST UNCOMFORTABLE

IF ever any one was sorry for having played pranks on other folks, that one was Peter Rabbit. I am afraid it wasn't quite the right kind of sorrow. You see, he wasn't sorry because of what had happened to Jimmy Skunk and Reddy Fox, but because of what had happened to himself. There he was, down in the bedroom of Johnny Chuck's old house, smarting and aching all over from the sharp little lances of the Yellow Jackets who had driven him down there before he had had a chance to see what happened to Reddy Fox. That was bad enough, but what troubled Peter more was the thought that he

couldn't get out without once again facing those hot-tempered Yellow Jackets.
Peter wished with all his might that he
had known about their home in Johnny
Chuck's old house before ever he
thought of hiding there.

But wishes of that kind are about the
most useless things in the world. They
wouldn't help him now. He had so
many aches and smarts that he didn't
see how he could stand a single one
more, and yet he couldn't see how he
was going to get out without receiving
several more. All at once he had a com-
forting thought. He remembered that
Johnny Chuck usually has a back door.
If that were the case here, he would be
all right. He would find out. Cau-
tiously he poked his head out of the snug
bedroom. There was the long hall down
which he had come. And there—yes,
Sir, there was another hall! It must be

the way to the back door. Carefully
Peter crept up it

"Funny," thought he, "that I don't
see any light ahead of me."

And then he bumped his nose. Yes,
Sir, Peter bumped his nose against the
end of that hall. You see, it was an old
house, and like most old houses it was
rather a tumble-down affair. Anyway,
the back door had been blocked with a
great stone, and the walls of the back
hall had fallen in. There was no way
out there. Sadly Peter backed out to
the little bedroom. He would wait until
night, and perhaps then the Yellow
Jackets would be asleep, and he could
steal out the front way without getting
any more stings. Meanwhile he would
try to get a nap and forget his aches and
pains.

Hardly had Peter curled up for that
nap when he heard a voice. It sounded

as if it came from a long way off, but he knew just where it came from. It came from the doorway of that old house. He knew, too, whose voice it was. It was Jimmy Skunk's voice.

"I know where you are, Peter Rabbit," said the voice. "And I know why you are hiding down there. I know, too, how it happened that I was rolled down hill in that barrel. I'm just giving you a little warning, Peter. There are a lot of very angry Yellow Jackets up here, as you will find out if you try to come out before dark. I'm going away now, but I'm going to come back about dark to wait for you. I may want to play a little joke on you to pay you back for the one you played on me."

That put an end to Peter's hope of a nap. He shivered as he thought of what might happen to him if Jimmy Skunk should catch him. What with his aches

and pains from the stings of the Yellow
Jackets, and fear of being caught by
Jimmy Skunk, it was quite impossible
to sleep. He was almost ready to face
those Yellow Jackets rather than wait
and meet Jimmy Skunk. Twice he
started up the long hall, but turned back.
He just couldn't stand any more stings.
He was miserable. Yes, Sir, he was
miserable and most uncomfortable in
both body and mind.

"I wish I'd never thought of that
joke," he half sobbed. "I thought it
was a great joke, but it wasn't. It was
a horrid, mean joke. Why, oh, why did
I ever think of it?"

Meanwhile Jimmy Skunk had gone
off, chuckling.

XI

Keep your word, whate'er you do,
And to your inmost self be true.

WHEN Jimmy Skunk shouted
down the hall of Johnny
Chuck's old house to Peter
Rabbit that he would come back at dark,
he was half joking. He did it to make
Peter uneasy and to worry him. The
truth is, Jimmy was no longer angry at
all. He had quite recovered his good
nature and was very much inclined to
laugh himself over Peter's trick. But
he felt that it wouldn't do to let Peter
off without some kind of punishment,
and so he decided to frighten Peter a
little. He knew that Peter wouldn't

dare come out during the daytime because of the Yellow Jackets whose home
was just inside the doorway of that old
house; and he knew that Peter wouldn't
dare face him, for he would be afraid of
being treated as Reddy Fox had been.
So that is why he told Peter that he was
coming back at dark. He felt that if
Peter was kept a prisoner in there for
a while, all the time worrying about how
he was to get out, he would be very slow
to try such a trick again.

As Jimmy ambled away to look for
some beetles, he chuckled and chuckled
and chuckled. "I guess that by this
time Peter wishes he hadn't thought of
that joke on Reddy Fox and myself,"
said he. "Perhaps I'll go back there
tonight and perhaps I won't. He won't
know whether I do or not, and he won't
dare come out."

Then he stopped and scratched his

head thoughtfully. Then he sighed.
Then he scratched his head again and
once more sighed. "I really don't want
to go back there tonight," he muttered,
"but I guess I'll have to. I said I
would, and so I'll have to do it. I believe in keeping my word. If I
shouldn't and some day he should find
it out, he wouldn't believe me the next
time I happened to say I would do a
thing. Yes, Sir, I'll have to go back.
There is nothing like making people believe that when you say a thing you
mean it. There is nothing like keeping
your word to make people respect you."

Being naturally rather lazy, Jimmy
decided not to go any farther than the
edge of the Old Orchard, which was only
a little way above Johnny Chuck's old
house, where Peter was a prisoner.
There Jimmy found a warm, sunny
spot and curled up for a nap. In fact,

he spent all the day there. When jolly, round, red Mr. Sun went to bed behind the Purple Hills, and the Black Shadows came trooping across the Green Meadows, Jimmy got up, yawned, chuckled, and then slowly ambled down to Johnny Chuck's old house. A look at the footprints in the sand on the doorstep told him that Peter had not come out. Jimmy sat down and waited until it was quite dark. Then he poked his head in at the doorway. The Yellow Jackets had gone to bed for the night.

"Come out, Peter. I'm waiting for you!" he called down the hall, and made his voice sound as angry as he could. But inside he was chuckling. Then Jimmy Skunk calmly turned and went about his business. He had kept his word.

As for Peter Rabbit, that had been one of the very worst days he could re-

call. He had ached and smarted from
the stings of the Yellow Jackets; he had
worried all day about what would happen to him if he did meet Jimmy Skunk,
and he was hungry. He had had just a
little bit of hope, and this was that
Jimmy Skunk wouldn't come back when
it grew dark. He had crept part way
up the hall at the first hint of night and
stretched himself out to wait until he
could be sure that those dreadful Yellow
Jackets had gone to sleep. He had just
about made up his mind that it was safe
for him to scamper out when Jimmy
Skunk's voice came down the hall to
him. Poor Peter! The sound of that
voice almost broke his heart.

"He has come back. He's kept his
word," he half sobbed as he once more
went back to Johnny Chuck's old bedroom.

There he stayed nearly all the rest of

the night, though his stomach was so
empty it ached.   Just before it was time
for Mr. Sun to rise, Peter ventured to
dash out of Johnny Chuck's old house.
He got past the home of the Yellow
Jackets safely, for they were not yet
awake.   With his heart in his mouth, he
sprang out of the doorway.   Jimmy
Skunk wasn't there.   With a sigh of relief, Peter started for the dear, safe Old
Briar-patch, lipperty-lipperty-lip, as
fast as he could go.

"I'll never, never play another joke,"
he said, over and over again as he ran.

XII

JIMMY SKUNK AND UNC' BILLY POSSUM MEET

JIMMY SKUNK ambled along down the Lone Little Path through the Green Forest. He didn't hurry. Jimmy never does hurry. Hurrying and worrying are two things he leaves for his neighbors. Now and then Jimmy stopped to turn over a bit of bark or a stick, hoping to find some fat beetles. But it was plain to see that he had something besides fat beetles on his mind.

Up the Lone Little Path through the Green Forest shuffled Unc' Billy Possum. He didn't hurry. It was too warm to hurry. Unlike Jimmy Skunk,

he does hurry sometimes, does Unc'
Billy, especially when he suspects that
Bowser the Hound is about. And sometimes Unc' Billy does worry. You see,
there are people who think that Unc'
Billy would make a very good dinner.
Unc' Billy doesn't think he would.
Anyway, he has no desire to have the
experiment tried. So occasionally,
when he discovers one of these people
who think he would make a good dinner,
he worries a little.

But just now Unc' Billy was neither
hurrying nor worrying. There was no
need of doing either, and Unc' Billy
never does anything that there is no need
of doing. So Unc' Billy shuffled up the
Lone Little Path, and Jimmy Skunk
ambled down the Lone Little Path, and
right at a bend in the Lone Little Path
they met.

Jimmy Skunk grinned. "Hello,

Unc' Billy!" said he. "Have you seen
any fat beetles this morning?"

Unc' Billy grinned. "Good mo'nin',
Brer Skunk," he replied. "Ah can't
rightly say Ah have. Ah had it on mah
mind to ask yo' the same thing."

Jimmy sat down and looked at Unc'
Billy with twinkling eyes. His grin
grew broader and became a chuckle.
"Unc' Billy," said he, "have you ever in
your life combed your hair or brushed
your coat?" You know Unc' Billy usually looks as if every hair was trying to
point in a different direction from every
other hair, while Jimmy Skunk always
appears as neat as if he spent half his
time brushing and smoothing his handsome black and white coat.

Unc' Billy's eyes twinkled. "Ah
reckons Ah did such a thing once or
twice when Ah was very small, Brer
Skunk," said he, without a trace of a

smile. "But it seems to me a powerful
waste of time. Ah have mo' important
things to worry about. By the way,
Brer Skunk, did yo' ever run away from
anybody in all your life?"

Jimmy looked surprised at the question. He scratched his head thoughtfully. "Not that I remember of," said
he after a little. "Most folks run away
from me," he added with a little throaty
chuckle. "Those who don't run away
always are polite and step aside. It
may be that when I was a very little
fellow and didn't know much about the
Great World and the people who live in
it, I might have run away from some
one, but if I did, I can't remember it.
Why do you ask, Unc' Billy?"

"Oh, no reason in particular, Brer
Skunk. No reason in particular. Only
Ah wonder sometimes if yo' ever realize
how lucky yo' are. If Ah never had to

worry about mah hungry neighbors, Ah reckons perhaps Ah might brush mah coat oftener." Unc' Billy's eyes twinkled more than ever.

"Worry," replied Jimmy Skunk sagely, "is the result of being unprepared. Anybody who is prepared has no occasion to worry. Just think it over, Unc' Billy."

It was Unc' Billy's turn to scratch his head thoughtfully. "Ah fear Ah don't quite get your meaning, Brer Skunk," said he.

"Sit down, Unc' Billy, and I'll explain," replied Jimmy.

XIII

JIMMY SKUNK EXPLAINS

You'll find this true where'er you go
That those prepared few troubles know.

"TO begin with, I am not such a very big fellow, am I?" said Jimmy.

"Ah reckons Ah knows a right smart lot of folks bigger than yo', Brer Skunk," replied Unc' Billy, with a grin. You know Jimmy Skunk really is a little fellow compared with some of his neighbors.

"And I haven't very long claws or very big teeth, have I?" continued Jimmy.

"Ah reckons mine are about as long and about as big," returned Unc' Billy, looking more puzzled than ever.

"But you never see anybody bothering me, do you?" went on Jimmy.

"No," replied Unc' Billy.

"And it's the same way with Prickly Porky the Porcupine. You never see anybody bothering him or offering to do him any harm, do you?" persisted Jimmy.

"No," replied Unc' Billy once more.

"Why?" demanded Jimmy.

Unc' Billy grinned broadly. "Ah reckons, Brer Skunk," said he, "that there isn't anybody wants to go fo' to meddle with yo' and Brer Porky. Ah reckons most folks knows what would happen if they did, and that yo' and Brer Porky are folks it's a sight mo' comfortable to leave alone. Leastways, Ah does. Ah ain't aiming fo' trouble with either of yo'. That li'l bag of scent yo' carry is cert'nly most powerful, Brer Skunk, and Ah isn't hankering to brush against those little spears Brer Porky is so free with. Ah knows when Ah's well off, and Ah reckons most folks feel the same way."

Jimmy Skunk chuckled. "One more question, Unc' Billy," said he. "Did you ever know me to pick a quarrel and use that bag of scent without being attacked?"

Unc' Billy considered for a few minutes. "Ah can't say Ah ever did,' he replied.

"And you never knew Prickly Porky to go hunting trouble either," declared Jimmy. "We don't either of us go hunting trouble, and trouble never comes hunting us, and the reason is that we both are always prepared for trouble and everybody knows it. Buster Bear could squash me by just stepping on me, but he doesn't try it. You notice he always is very polite when we meet.

Prickly Porky and I are armed for *defence,* but we never use our weapons for *offence.* Nobody bothers us, and we bother nobody. That's the beauty of being prepared."

Unc' Billy thought it over for a few minutes. Then he sighed and sighed again.

"Ah reckons yo' and Brer Porky are about the luckiest people Ah knows," said he. "Yes, Sah, Ah reckons yo' is just that. Ah don't fear anybody mah own size, but Ah cert'nly does have some mighty scary times when Ah meets some people Ah might mention. Ah wish Ol' Mother Nature had done gone and given me something fo' to make people as scary of me as they are of yo'. Ah cert'nly believes in preparedness after seein yo', Brer Skunk. Ah cert'nly does just that very thing. Have yo' found any nice fresh aiggs lately?"

XIV

A LITTLE SOMETHING ABOUT EGGS

"An egg," says Jimmy Skunk, "is good;
  It's very good indeed to eat."
"An egg," says Mrs. Grouse, "is dear;
  'Twill hatch into a baby sweet."

SO in the matter of eggs, as in a great
many other matters, it all depends
on the point of view. To Jimmy
Skunk and Unc' Billy Possum eggs are
looked on from the viewpoint of something to eat. Their stomachs prompt
them to think of eggs. Eggs are good
to fill empty stomachs. The mere
thought of eggs will make Jimmy and
Unc' Billy smack their lips. They say
they "love" eggs, but they don't. They
"like" them, which is quite different.

But Mrs. Grouse and most of the other feathered people of the Green Forest and the Green Meadows and the Old Orchard really do "love" eggs. It is the heart instead of the stomach that responds to the thought of eggs. To them eggs are almost as precious as babies, because they know that some day, some day very soon, those eggs will become babies. There are a few feathered folks, I am sorry to say, who "love" their own eggs, but "like" the eggs of other people—like them just as Jimmy Skunk and Unc' Billy Possum do, to eat. Blacky the Crow is one and his cousin, Sammy Jay, is another.

So in the springtime there is always a great deal of matching of wits between the little people of the Green Forest and the Green Meadows and the Old Orchard. Those who have eggs try to keep them a secret or to build the nests that hold them where none who like to eat them can get them; and those who have an appetite for eggs try to find them.

When Unc' Billy Possum suddenly changed the subject by asking Jimmy Skunk if he had found any nice fresh eggs lately, he touched a subject very close to Jimmy's heart. I should have said, rather, his stomach. To tell the truth, it was a longing for some eggs that had brought Jimmy to the Green Forest. He knew that somewhere there Mrs. Grouse must be hiding a nestful of the very nicest of eggs, and it was to hunt for these that he had come.

"No," replied Jimmy, "I haven't had any luck at all this spring. I've almost forgotten what an egg tastes like. Either I'm growing dull and stupid, or some folks are smarter than they used to be. By the way, have you seen Mrs.

Grouse lately?" Jimmy looked very innocent as he asked this.

Unc' Billy chuckled until his sides shook. "Do yo' suppose Ah'd tell yo' if Ah had?" he demanded. "Ah reckons Mrs. Grouse hasn't got any mo' aiggs than Ah could comfortably take care of mahself, not to mention Mrs. Possum." Here Unc' Billy looked back over his shoulder to make sure that old Mrs. Possum wasn't within hearing, and Jimmy Skunk chuckled. "Seems to me, Brer Skunk, yo' might better do your aigg hunting on the Green Meadows and leave the Green Forest to me," continued Unc' Billy. "That would be no mo' than fair. Yo' know Ah never did hanker fo' to get far away from trees, but yo' don't mind. Besides there are mo' aiggs for yo' to find on the Green Meadows than there are fo' me to find in the Green Forest. A righ*

smart lot of birds make their nests on
the ground there. There is Brer Bob
White and Brer Meadowlark and Brer
Bobolink and Brer Field Sparrow and
Brer—"

"Never mind any more, Unc' Billy,"
interrupted Jimmy Skunk. "I know
all about them. That is, I know all
about them I want to know, except
where their eggs are. Didn't I just tell
you I haven't had any luck at all?
That's why I'm over here."

"Well, yo' won't have any mo' luck
here unless yo' are a right smart lot
sharper than your Unc' Billy, and when
it comes to hunting aiggs, Ah don't take
mah hat off to anybody, not even to yo',
Brer Skunk," replied Unc' Billy.

XV

A SECOND MEETING

JIMMY SKUNK couldn't think of anything but eggs. The more he thought of them, the more he wanted some. After parting from Unc' Billy Possum in the Green Forest he went back to the Green Meadows and prowled about, hunting for the nests of his feathered neighbors who build on the ground, and having no more luck than he had had before.

Unc' Billy Possum was faring about the same way. He couldn't, for the life of him, stop thinking about those eggs that belonged to Mrs. Grouse. The more he tried to forget about them, the more he thought about them.

"Ah feels it in mah bones that there isn't the least bit of use in huntin' fo' them," said he to himself, as he watched Jimmy Skunk amble out of sight up the Lone Little Path. "No, Sah, there isn't the least bit of use. Ah done look every place Ah can think of already. Still, Ah haven't got anything else special on mah mind, and those aiggs cert'nly would taste good. Ah reckons it must be Ah needs those aiggs, or Ah wouldn't have them on mah mind so much. Ah finds it rather painful to carry aiggs on mah mind all the time, but Ah would enjoy carrying them in mah stomach. Ah cert'nly would." Unc' Billy grinned and started to ramble about aimlessly, hoping that chance would lead him to the nest of Mrs. Grouse.

Do what he would, Unc' Billy couldn't get the thought of eggs off his mind, and the more he thought about them the

more he wanted some. And that led
him to think of Farmer Brown's henhouse. He had long ago resolved never
again to go there, but the longing for a
taste of eggs was too much for his good
resolutions, and as soon as jolly, round,
red Mr. Sun sank to rest behind the Purple Hills, and the Black Shadows came
creeping across the Green Meadows and
through the Green Forest, Unc' Billy
slipped away, taking pains that old
Mrs. Possum shouldn't suspect where he
was going.

Out from the Green Forest, keeping
among the Black Shadows along by the
old stone wall on the edge of the Old
Orchard, he stole, and so at last he
reached Farmer Brown's henhouse.
He stopped to listen. There was no
sign of Bowser the Hound, and Unc'
Billy sighed gently. It was a sigh of
relief. Then he crept around a corner

of the henhouse towards a certain hole under it he remembered well. Just as he reached it, he saw something white. It moved. It was coming towards him from the other end of the henhouse. Unc' Billy stopped right where he was. He was undecided whether to run or stay. Then he heard a little grunt and decided to stay. He even grinned. A few seconds later up came Jimmy Skunk. It was a white stripe on Jimmy's coat that Unc' Billy had seen.

Jimmy gave a little snort of surprise when he almost bumped into Unc' Billy.

"What are you doing here?" he demanded.

"Just taking a li'l walk fo' the good of mah appetite," replied Unc' Billy, grinning more broadly than ever. "What are yo' doing here, Brer Skunk?"

"The same thing," replied Jimmy.

Then he chuckled. "This is an unexpected meeting. I guess you must have had the same thing on your mind all day that I have," he added.

"Ah reckon so," replied Unc' Billy, and both grinned.

XVI

A MATTER OF POLITENESS

It costs not much to be polite
And, furthermore, it's always right.

UNC' BILLY POSSUM and
Jimmy Skunk, facing each
other among the Black Shadows
close by a hole that led under Farmer
Brown's henhouse, chuckled as each
thought of what had brought the other
there. It is queer how a like thought
often brings people together. Unc'
Billy had the same longing in his stomach that Jimmy Skunk had, and Jimmy
Skunk had the same thing on his mind
that Unc' Billy had. More than this,
it was the second time that day that
they had met. They had met in the

morning in the Green Forest and now
they had met again among the Black
Shadows of the evening at Farmer
Brown's henhouse. And it was all on
account of eggs. Yes, Sir, it was all on
account of eggs.

"Are you just coming out, or are you
just going in?" Jimmy inquired politely.

"Ah was just going in, but Ah'll follow yo', Brer Skunk," replied Unc'
Billy just as politely.

"Nothing of the kind," returned
Jimmy. "I wouldn't for a minute
think of going before you. I hope I
know my manners better than that."

"Yo' cert'nly are most polite, Brer
Skunk. Yo' cert'nly are most polite.
Yo' are a credit to your bringing up, but
politeness always did run in your family. There is a saying that han'some is
as han'some does, and your politeness

is as fine as yo' are han'some, Brer Skunk. Ah'll just step one side and let yo' go first just to show that Ah sho'ly does appreciate your friendship," said Unc' Billy.

Jimmy Skunk chuckled. "I guess you've forgotten that other old saying, 'Age before beauty,' Unc' Billy," said he. "So you go first. You know you are older than I. I couldn't think of being so impolite as to go first. I really couldn't think of such a thing."

And so they argued and argued, each insisting in the most polite way that the other should go first. If the truth were known, neither of them was insisting out of politeness at all. No, Sir, politeness had nothing to do with it. Jimmy Skunk wanted Unc' Billy to go first because Jimmy believes in safety first, and it had popped into Jimmy's head that there might, there just might, happen to be a trap inside that hole. If there was, he much preferred that Unc' Billy should be the one to find it out. Yes, Sir, that is why Jimmy Skunk was so very polite.

Unc' Billy wanted Jimmy to go first because he always feels safer behind Jimmy than in front of him. He has great respect for that little bag of scent that Jimmy carries, and he knows that when Jimmy makes use of it, he always throws it in front and never behind him. Jimmy seldom uses it, but sometimes he does if he happens to be startled and thinks danger near. So Unc' Billy preferred that Jimmy should go first. It wasn't politeness at all on the part of Unc' Billy. In both cases it was a kind of selfishness. Each was thinking of self.

How long they would have continued to argue and try to appear polite if something hadn't happened, nobody knows. But something did happen. There was a sudden loud sniff just around the corner of the henhouse. It was from Bowser the Hound. Right then and there Unc' Billy Possum and Jimmy Skunk forgot all about politeness, and both tried to get through that hole at the same time. They couldn't, because it wasn't big enough, but, they tried hard. Bowser sniffed again, and this time Unc' Billy managed to squeeze Jimmy aside and slip through. Jimmy was right at his heels.

XVII

JIMMY SKUNK GETS A BUMP

HARDLY had Jimmy Skunk entered the hole under Farmer Brown's henhouse, following close on the heels of Unc' Billy Possum, than along came Bowser the Hound, sniffing and sniffing in a way that made Unc' Billy nervous. When Bowser reached that hole, of course he smelled the tracks of Unc' Billy and Jimmy, and right away he became excited. He began to dig. Goodness, how he did make the dirt fly! All the time he whined with eagerness.

Unc' Billy wasted no time in squeezing through a hole in the floor way over

in one corner, a hole that Farmer
Brown's boy had intended to nail a
board over long before. Unc' Billy
knew that Bowser couldn't get through
that, even if he did manage to dig his
way under the henhouse. Once through
that and fairly in the henhouse, Unc'
Billy drew a long breath. He felt safe
for the time being, anyway, and he
didn't propose to worry over the future.

Jimmy Skunk hurried after Unc'
Billy. It wasn't fear that caused
Jimmy to hurry. No, indeed, it wasn't
fear. He had been startled by the un-
expectedness of Bowser's appearance.
It was this that had caused him to strug-
gle to be first through that hole under
the henhouse. But once through, he
had felt a bit ashamed that he had been
so undignified. He wasn't afraid of
Bowser. He was sorely tempted to turn
around and send Bowser about his busi-

ness, as he knew he very well could.
But he thought better of it. Besides,
Unc' Billy was already through that
hole in the floor, and Jimmy didn't for
a minute forget what had brought him
there. He had come for eggs, and so
had Unc' Billy. It would never do to
let Unc' Billy be alone up there for
long. So Jimmy Skunk did what he
very seldom does—hurried. Yes, Sir,
he hurried after Unc' Billy Possum.
He meant to make sure of his share of
the eggs he was certain were up there.

There was a row of nesting boxes
along one side close to the floor. Above
these was another row and above these
a third row. Jimmy doesn't climb, but
Unc' Billy is a famous climber.

"I'll take these lower nests," said
Jimmy, and lifted his tail in a way that
made Unc' Billy nervous.

"All right," replied Unc' Billy

promptly. "All right, Brer Skunk.
It's just as yo' say."

With this, Unc' Billy scrambled up to
the next row of nests. Jimmy grinned
and started to look in the lower nests.
He took his time about it, for that is
Jimmy's way. There was nothing in
the first one and nothing in the second
one and nothing in the third one. This
was disappointing, to say the least, and
Jimmy began to move a little faster.
Meanwhile Unc' Billy had hurried from
one nest to another in the second row
with no better success. By the time
Jimmy was half-way along his row Unc'
Billy had begun on the upper row, and
the only eggs he had found were hard
china nest-eggs put there by Farmer
Brown's boy to tempt the hens to lay in
those particular nests. Disappointment was making Unc' Billy lose his
temper. Each time he peeped in a nest

and saw one of those china eggs, he
hoped it was a real egg, and each time
when he found it wasn't he grew angrier.

At last he so lost his temper that when
he found another of those eggs he an-
grily kicked it out of the nest. Now it
happened that Jimmy Skunk was just
underneath. Down fell that hard china
egg squarely on Jimmy Skunk's head.
For just a minute Jimmy saw stars.
At least, he thought he did. Then he
saw the egg, and knew that Unc' Billy
had knocked it down, and that it was
this that had hit him. Jimmy was sore
at heart because he had found no eggs,
and now he had a bump on the head that
also was sore. Jimmy Skunk lost his
temper, a thing he rarely does.

XVIII

A SAD, SAD QUARREL

JIMMY SKUNK sat on the floor of
Farmer Brown's henhouse, rubbing
his head and glaring up at the upper row of nests with eyes red with anger. Of course it was dark in the henhouse, for it was night, but Jimmy can
see in the dark, just as so many other
little people who wear fur can. What
he saw was the anxious looking face of
Unc' Billy Possum staring down at him.

"You did that purposely!" snapped
Jimmy. "You did that purposely, and
you needn't tell me you didn't."

"On mah honor Ah didn't," protested
Unc' Billy. "It was an accident, just
a sho' 'nuff accident, and Ah'm right
sorry fo' it."

"That sounds very nice, but I don't believe a word of it. You did it purposely, and you can't make me believe anything else. Come down here and fight. I dare you to!" Jimmy was getting more and more angry every minute.

Unc' Billy began to grow angry. Of course, it was wholly his fault that that egg had fallen, but it wasn't his fault that Jimmy had happened to be just beneath. He hadn't known that Jimmy was there. He had apologized, and he felt that no one could do more than that. Jimmy Skunk had doubted his word, had refused to believe him, and that made him angry. His little eyes glowed with rage.

"If yo' want to fight, come up here. I'll wait fo' yo' right where Ah am," he sputtered.

This made Jimmy angrier than ever.

He couldn't climb up there, and he knew that Unc' Billy knew it. Unc' Billy was perfectly safe in promising to wait for him.

"You're a coward, just a plain no-account coward!" snapped Jimmy. "I'm not going to climb up there, but I'll tell you what I am going to do; I'm going to wait right down here until you come down, if it isn't until next year. Nobody can drop things on my head and not get paid back. I thought you were a friend, but now I know better."

"Wait as long as yo' please. Ah reckons Ah can stay as long as yo' can," retorted Unc' Billy, grinding and snapping his teeth.

"Suit yourself," retorted Jimmy. "I'm going to pay you up for that bump on my head or know the reason why."

And so they kept on quarreling and calling each other names, for the time

being quite forgetting that they were
where they had no business to be, either
of them. It really was dreadful. And
it was all because both had been sadly
disappointed. They had found no eggs
where they had been sure they would
find plenty. You see, Farmer Brown's
boy had gathered every egg when he
shut the biddies up for the night. Did
you ever notice what a bad thing for the
temper disappointment often is?

XIX

U NC' BILLY POSSUM was having a bad night of it. When he had grown tired of quarreling with Jimmy Skunk, he had tried to take a nap. He had tried first one nest and then another, but none just suited him. This was partly because he wasn't sleepy. He was hungry and not at all sleepy. He wished with all his heart that he hadn't foolishly yielded to that fit of temper which had resulted in kicking that china nest-egg out of a nest and down on the head of Jimmy Skunk, making Jimmy so thoroughly angry.

Unc' Billy had no intention of going down while Jimmy was there. He thought that Jimmy would soon grow tired of waiting and go away. So for quite awhile Unc' Billy didn't worry. But as it began to get towards morning he began to grow anxious. Unc' Billy had no desire to be found in that hen-house when Farmer Brown's boy came to feed the biddies.

Then, too, he was hungry. He had counted on a good meal of eggs, and not one had he found. Now he wanted to get out to look for something else to eat, but he couldn't without facing Jimmy Skunk, and it was better to go hungry than to do that. Yes, Sir, it was a great deal better to go hungry. Several times, when he thought Jimmy was asleep, he tried to steal down. He was just as careful not to make a sound as he could be, but every time Jimmy knew and was waiting for him. Unc' Billy wished that there was no such

place as Farmer Brown's henhouse.
He wished he had never thought of
eggs. He wished many other foolish
wishes, but most of all he wished that
he hadn't lost his temper and kicked
that egg down on Jimmy Skunk's head.
When the first light stole in under the
door and the biddies began to stir un-
easily on their roosts Unc' Billy's
anxiety would allow him to keep still no
longer.

"Don' yo' think we-uns better make
up and get out of here, Brer Skunk?"
he ventured.

"I don't mind staying here; it's very
comfortable," replied Jimmy, looking
up at Unc' Billy in a way that made him
most *uncomfortable*. It was plain to
see that Jimmy hadn't forgiven him.

For some time Unc' Billy said no
more, but he grew more and more rest-
less. You see, he knew it would soon be

time for Farmer Brown's boy to come to let the hens out and feed them. At last he ventured to speak again.

"Ah reckons yo' done forget something," said he.

"What is that?" asked Jimmy.

"Ah reckons yo' done fo'get that it's most time fo' Farmer Brown's boy to come, and it won't do fo' we-uns to be found in here," replied Unc' Billy.

"I'm not worrying about Farmer Brown's boy. He can come as soon as he pleases," retorted Jimmy Skunk, and grinned.

That sounded like boasting, but it wasn't. No, Sir, it wasn't, and Unc' Billy knew it. He knew that Jimmy meant it. Unc' Billy was in despair. He didn't dare stay, and he didn't dare go down and face Jimmy Skunk, and there he was. It certainly had been a bad night for Unc' Billy Possum.

XX

FARMER BROWN'S BOY ARRIVES

THE light crept farther under the door of Farmer Brown's henhouse, and by this time the hens were all awake. Furthermore, they had discovered Jimmy Skunk down below and were making a great fuss. They were cackling so that Unc' Billy was sure Farmer Brown's boy would soon hear them and hurry out to find out what the noise was all about.

"If yo' would just get out of sight, Brer Skunk, Ah reckons those fool hens would keep quiet," Unc' Billy ventured.

"I don't mind their noise. It doesn't

trouble me a bit,'' replied Jimmy Skunk,
and grinned. It was plain enough to
Unc' Billy that Jimmy was enjoying
the situation.

But Unc' Billy wasn't. He was so
anxious that he couldn't keep still. He
paced back and forth along the shelf in
front of the upper row of nests and
tried to make up his mind whether it
would be better to go down and face
Jimmy Skunk or to try to hide under
the hay in one of the nests, and all the
time he kept listening and listening and
listening for the footsteps of Farmer
Brown's boy.

At last he heard them, and he knew
by the sound that Farmer Brown's boy
was coming in a hurry. He had heard
the noise of the hens and was coming to
find out what it was all about. Unc'
Billy hoped that now Jimmy Skunk
would retreat through the hole in the

floor and give him a chance to escape.

"He's coming! Farmer Brown's boy is coming, Brer Skunk! Yo' better get away while yo' can!" whispered Unc' Billy.

"I hear him," replied Jimmy calmly. "I'm waiting for him to open the door for me to go out. It will be much easier than squeezing through that hole."

Unc' Billy gasped. He knew, of course, that it was Jimmy Skunk's boast that he feared no one, but it was hard to believe that Jimmy really intended to face Farmer Brown's boy right in his own henhouse where Jimmy had no business to be. He hoped that at last Jimmy's boldness would get him into trouble. Yes, he did. You see, that might give him a chance to slip away himself. Otherwise, he would be in a bad fix.

The latch on the door rattled. Unc'

Billy crept into one of the nests, but frightened as he was, he couldn't keep from peeping over the edge to see what would happen. The door swung open, letting in a flood of light. The hens stopped their noise. Farmer Brown's boy stood in the doorway and looked in. Jimmy Skunk lifted his big plume of a tail just a bit higher than usual and calmly and without the least sign of being in a hurry walked straight towards the open door. Of course Farmer Brown's boy saw him at once.

"So it's you, you black and white rascal!" he exclaimed. "I suppose you expect me to step out of your way, and I suppose I will do just that very thing. You are the most impudent and independent fellow of my acquaintance. That's what you are. You didn't get any eggs, because I gathered all of them last night. And you didn't get a chicken because they were wise enough to stay on their roosts, so I don't know as I have any quarrel with you, and I'm sure I don't want any. Come along out of there, you rascal."

Farmer Brown's boy stepped aside, and Jimmy Skunk calmly and without the least sign of hurry or worry walked out, stopped for a drink at the pan of water in the henyard, walked through the henyard gate, and turned towards the stone wall along the edge of the Old Orchard.

XXI

THE NEST-EGG GIVES UNC' BILLY AWAY

> 'Tis little things that often seem
> Scarce worth a passing thought
> Which in the end may prove that they
> With big results are fraught.

FARMER BROWN'S boy watched Jimmy Skunk calmly and peacefully go his way and grinned as he watched him. He scratched his head thoughtfully. "I suppose," said he, "that that is as perfect an example of the value of preparedness as there is. Jimmy knew he was all ready for trouble if I chose to make it, and that because of that I wouldn't make it. So he has calmly gone his way as if he were as much bigger than I as I am bigger than he. There certainly is nothing like being prepared if you want to avoid trouble.''

Then Farmer Brown's boy once more turned to the henhouse and entered it. He looked to make sure that no hen had been foolish enough to go to sleep where Jimmy could have caught her, and satisfied of this, he would have gone about his usual morning work of feeding the hens but for one thing. That one thing was the china nest-egg on the floor.

''Hello!'' exclaimed Farmer Brown's boy when he saw it. ''Now how did that come there? It must be that Jimmy Skunk pulled it out of one of those lower nests.''

Now he knew just which nests had contained nest-eggs, and it didn't take but a minute to find that none was missing in any of the lower nests. ''That's queer,'' he muttered. ''That egg must

have come from one of the upper nests.
Jimmy couldn't have got up to those.
None of the hens could have kicked it
out last night, because they were all on
the roosts when I shut them up. They
certainly didn't do it this morning, because they wouldn't have dared leave
the roosts with Jimmy Skunk here.
I'll have to look into this."

So he began with the second row of
nests and looked in each. Then he
started on the upper row, and so he
came to the nest in which Unc' Billy
Possum was hiding under the hay and
holding his breath. Now Unc' Billy
had covered himself up pretty well with
the hay, but he had forgotten one thing;
he had forgotten his tail. Yes, Sir,
Unc' Billy had forgotten his tail, and it
hung just over the edge of the nest. Of
course, Farmer Brown's boy saw it.
He couldn't help but see it.

"Ho, ho!" he exclaimed right away. "Ho, ho! So there was more than one visitor here last night. This henhouse seems to be a very popular place. I see that the first thing for me to do after breakfast is to nail a board over that hole in the floor. So it was you, Unc' Billy Possum, who kicked that nest-egg out. Found it a little hard for your teeth, didn't you? Lost your temper and kicked it out, didn't you? That was foolish, Unc' Billy, very foolish indeed. Never lose your temper over trifles. It doesn't pay. Now I wonder what I'd better do with you."

All this time Unc' Billy hadn't moved. Of course, he couldn't understand what Farmer Brown's boy was saying. Nor could he see what Farmer Brown's boy was doing. So he held his breath and hoped and hoped that he hadn't been discovered. And perhaps he wouldn't

have been but for that telltale nest-egg
on the floor. That was the cause of all
his troubles. First it had angered
Jimmy Skunk because as you remember, it had fallen on Jimmy's head.
Then it had led Farmer Brown's boy to
look in all the nests. It had seemed a
trifle, kicking that egg out of that nest,
but see what the results were. Truly,
little things often are not so little as
they seem.

XXII

THE first knowledge Unc' Billy Possum had that he was discovered came to him through his tail. Yes, Sir, it came to him through his tail. Farmer Brown's boy pinched it. It was rather a mean thing to do, but Farmer Brown's boy was curious. He wanted to see what Unc' Billy would do. And he didn't pinch very hard, not hard enough to really hurt. Farmer Brown's boy is too good-hearted to hurt any one if he can help it.

Now any other of the Green Forest and Green Meadows people would promptly have pulled their tail away had they been in Unc' Billy's place

But Unc' Billy didn't. No, Sir, Unc' Billy didn't. That tail might have belonged to any one but him so far as he made any sign. Of course, he felt like pulling it away. Any one would have in his place. But he didn't move it the tiniest bit, which goes to show that Unc' Billy has great self-control when he wishes.

Farmer Brown's boy pinched again, just a little harder, but still Unc' Billy made no sign. Farmer Brown's boy chuckled and began to pull on that tail. He pulled and pulled until finally he had pulled Unc' Billy out of his hiding-place, and he swung by his tail from the hand of Farmer Brown's boy. There wasn't the least sign of life about Unc' Billy. He looked as if he were dead, and he acted as if he were dead. Any one not knowing Unc' Billy would have supposed that he *was* dead.

Farmer Brown's boy dropped Unc' Billy on the floor. He lay just as he fell. Farmer Brown's boy rolled him over with his foot, but there wasn't a sign of life in Unc' Billy. He hoped that Farmer Brown's boy really did think him dead. That was what he wanted. Farmer Brown's boy picked him up again and laid him on a box, first putting a board over the hole in the floor and closing the henhouse door. Then he went about his work of cleaning out the henhouse and measuring out the grain for the biddies.

Unc' Billy lay there on the box, and he certainly was pathetic looking. A dead animal or bird is always pathetic looking, and none was ever more so than Unc' Billy Possum as he lay on that box. His hair was all rumpled up, as it usually is. It was filled with dust from the floor and bits of straw. His lips

were drawn back and his mouth partly
open. His eyes seemed to be closed.
As a matter of fact, they were open just
a teeny, weeny bit, just enough for Unc'
Billy to watch Farmer Brown's boy.
But to have looked at him you would
have thought him as dead as the deadest
thing that ever was.

As he went about his work Farmer
Brown's boy kept an eye on Unc' Billy
and chuckled. "You old fraud," said
he. "You think you are fooling me, but
I know you. Possums don't die of
nothing in hens' nests. You certainly
are a clever old rascal, and the best ac-
tor I've ever seen. I wonder how long
you will keep it up. I wish I had half
as much self-control."

When he had finished his work he
picked Unc' Billy up by the tail once
more, opened the door, and started for
the house with Unc' Billy swinging from

his hand and bumping against his legs. Still Unc' Billy gave no sign of life. He wondered where he was being taken to. He was terribly frightened. But he stuck to his old trick of playing dead which had served him so well more than once before.

XXIII

UNC' BILLY GIVES HIMSELF AWAY

NEVER had Unc' Billy Possum played that old trick of his better than he was playing it now. Farmer Brown's boy knew that Unc' Billy was only pretending to be dead, yet so well did Unc' Billy pretend that it was hard work for Farmer Brown's boy to believe what he knew was the truth—that Unc' Billy was very much alive and only waiting for a chance to slip away.

They were half-way from the henyard to the house when Bowser the Hound came to meet his master. "Now we shall see what we shall see," said Farmer Brown's boy, as Bowser came

trotting up. "If Unc' Billy can stand
this test, I'll take off my hat to him
every time we meet hereafter." He
held Unc' Billy out to Bowser, and
Bowser sniffed him all over.

Just imagine that! Just think of being nosed and sniffed at by one of whom
you were terribly afraid and not so
much as twitching an ear! Farmer
Brown's boy dropped Unc' Billy on the
ground, and Bowser rolled him over and
sniffed at him and then looked up at his
master, as much as to say: "This fellow doesn't interest me. He's dead.
He must be the fellow I saw go under
the henhouse last night. How did you
kill him?"

Farmer Brown's boy laughed and
picked Unc' Billy up by the tail again.
"He's fooled you all right, old fellow,
and you don't know it," said he to Bowser, as the latter pranced on ahead to

the house. The mother of Farmer Brown's boy was in the doorway, watching them approach.

"What have you got there?" she demanded. "I declare if it isn't a Possum! Where did you kill him? Was he the cause of all that racket among the chickens?"

Farmer Brown's boy took Unc' Billy into the kitchen and dropped him on a chair. Mrs. Brown came over to look at him closer. "Poor little fellow," said she. "Poor little fellow. It was too bad he got into mischief and had to be killed. I don't suppose he knew any better. Somehow it always seems wrong to me to kill these little creatures just because they get into mischief when all the time they don't know that they are in mischief." She stroked Unc' Billy gently.

The eyes of Farmer Brown's boy

twinkled. He went over to a corner
and pulled a straw from his mother's
broom. Then he returned to Unc' Billy
and began to tickle Unc' Billy's nose.
Mrs. Brown looked puzzled. She was
puzzled.

"What are you doing that for?" she
asked.

"Just for fun," replied Farmer
Brown's boy and kept on tickling Unc'
Billy's nose. Now Unc' Billy could
stand having his tail pinched, and being
carried head down, and being dropped
on the ground, but this was too much for
him; he wanted to sneeze. He had *got*
to sneeze. He did sneeze. He couldn't
help it, though it were to cost him his
life.

"Land of love!" exclaimed Mrs.
Brown, jumping back and clutching her
skirts in both hands as if she expected
Unc' Billy would try to take refuge be-

hind them. "Do you mean to say that that Possum is alive?"

"Seems that way," replied Farmer Brown's boy as Unc' Billy sneezed again, for that straw was still tickling his nose. "I should certainly say it seems that way. The old sinner is no more dead than I am. He's just pretending. He fooled you all right, Mother, but he didn't fool me. I haven't hurt a hair of him. You ought to know me well enough by this time to know that I wouldn't hurt him."

He looked at his mother reproachfully, and she hastened to apologize. "But what could I think?" she demanded. "If he isn't a dead-looking creature, I never have seen one. What are you going to do with him, son?"

"Take him over to the Green Forest after breakfast and let him go," replied Farmer Brown's boy.

This is just what he did do, and Unc' Billy wasted no time in getting home. It was a long time before he met Jimmy Skunk again. When he did, Jimmy was his usual good-natured self, and Unc' Billy was wise enough not to refer to eggs.

THE END